Still His

Woman

An Against the Odds Novelette

J. Adams

J. Adams

To all the mothers I know,
both with children and without.

Chapter 1

Snap out of it, girl! Stop doing this because it doesn't matter.

For the last three months, I have mentally repeated this affirmation too many times to count, and I can't seem to stop. Ever since the day I underwent a complete hysterectomy because of diagnosed ovarian cancer, there has been a subtle shift in my brain and emotions. I'm grateful we were able to catch it soon enough to avoid chemotherapy. The cancer had been isolated and hadn't spread to my blood at all. I'm thankful to still be here with Hayden and our children—but I feel as if I have lost a part of me.

Folding another load of freshly dried clothes, I smile sadly as I again think of our dream to fill the house with children. I love Dane and Maggie more than I can say, and though I'm grateful beyond words to have them, I always thought there would be more children. Dane is seven and Maggie is five. We've tried for years to have another baby.

Now it's no longer possible.

Heaving a deep sigh, I pick up the basket of clean clothes and take them and put them all away. I grab a blanket from the closet, and then head to the kitchen to pack the lunch I prepared for Hayden and me in a leather messenger bag. After putting the blanket and the bag in the SUV, I round up the kids and take them down to their Aunt Caroline at the main house to hang out with her for a while. She always enjoys having them there and usually plans fun activities to keep them busy.

I quietly slip into the barn. Hayden's bare back is to me. He sits on a large stump, lifting his arms over his head, stretching his massive, muscular six-foot-eleven inch frame. Just watching him casually talking to the hired hands produces butterflies inside my stomach and a familiar warmth spreads through my body. We've been married for seven years and he still affects me the same way.

Tom and the rest of the men glance at me and I hold a finger to my lips, urging them to say nothing. I am very fond of the men who work with Hayden. And except for the new worker they hired last week, the rest have been in Hayden and his brother David's employ for years, long before I came to Roswell.

"Hey, Jack," Tom says, winking at me, "Hayden started growing soft as soon as he got married. He can hardly keep up anymore." The guys laugh and I cover my mouth, muffling a giggle. The new guy grins widely, keeping his eyes on me, and his stare is slightly unnerving.

"Don't I know it," Hayden says with a warmth that pierces my heart. "I ain't gonna deny it. If you had a beautiful and incredible woman like mine, you'd be the same way."

Tom laughs. "See what I mean? When them two are together, they can't keep their hands off each other."

"Yeah," another man put in, "Hayden's dead on his feet half the time, and it ain't from working, if you catch my drift."

"But there's always a smile on his face," Tom adds.

Hayden rakes his fingers through his hair, combing the chestnut locks back from his face. "You guys are jealous. Admit it."

"You got me," Tom says, chuckling. "You think I could steal her away from ya?"

"When hell freezes over," Hayden answers with a playful growl that is only amplified by the deep, rich drawl I love so much.

Unable to wait another minute to touch him, I quietly approach and wrap my arms around his neck, soaking in his warmth and catching him by surprise. "Hey," I whisper against his ear.

"Hey, baby."

It doesn't matter what he says to me, his voice is always both soothing and seductive. Of course everything about him is seductive, with no effort on his part. It's just a fact.

"Ready to be kidnapped?" I press my face against his groomed, bearded cheek.

"By you?" he says, pulling me around to sit on his lap. "You know it."

"Can you guys do without him for a bit?"

"Yeah," Tom says. "He never does much, anyway."

Hayden rolls his eyes. "Can you believe them?"

"Yes, I can," I answer with a soft chuckle. "Hey, stop giving my husband a hard time. You're setting a bad example for this guy." I gesture to the new man.

"Thanks, for having my back, darlin'. Oh, this is Jack. Jack, my wife, Raine."

"It's nice to meet you, Jack."

"Good to meet you too," Jack says, tipping his hat. He casually lets his eyes roam over me, making me feel uncomfortable. No one else seems to notice. "You've got a beautiful wife, Hayden."

"I do indeed," Hayden agrees, kissing my cheek.

"Let's go." I stand, taking his hand. "I promise not to keep him long."

"May as well keep him," Tom says. "He won't be fit to do any work anyway." The other men laugh.

Hayden puts his gray t-shirt back on and grabs his hat. "We'll see who outworks who when I get back." He grins, taking my hand again. "Come on, darlin'. Let's get you out of this den of iniquity."

Tom and the rest of the men hoot loudly as we leave.

Chapter 2

Hayden

Hayden's hands circle Raine's waist and he effortlessly lifts her onto the horse. Even at five-foot-nine, she has always seemed so little to him, so breakable. He smiles up at her, taking in the way her long spiraled locks shine in the sun, the way her brown skin shimmers. He has never seen a more beautiful woman, and when she looks at him this way, with brown eyes so full of love, he goes weak in the knees.

His hat masks the anger that creases his brow as he thinks about the way Jack stared at his wife, undressing her with his eyes, as if he had a right to her. If they had stayed any longer, Hayden would most likely have lost his temper and seriously hurt the man.

Putting a foot up in the stirrup, he swings into the saddle behind her, loving the feel of her back pressed against his chest as they ride, relishing the touch of her slender hands gripping his thighs, the scent of her hair, and the smell of her perfume when he kisses her neck. Simply put, she is everything to him. And he feels an urgent need to be alone with her. They can't reach their destination fast enough.

Reaching our usual spot among a shady grove of trees, Hayden slips down from the horse and helps me down, keeping his hands on my waist, pulling me firmly against him. The moment he lowers his mouth to mine and begins his heated, passionate exploration, the lunch bag slips from my hands as a different hunger fills me, making me oblivious to the world around us. He releases me long enough to slip out of his shirt again before fully reclaiming me.

Passion soon finds us wrapped in the blanket, tangled up in one another, expressing our ever-growing love in words and actions that can never be denied. Surely there has never existed a pair of arms more heavenly than his, or two bodies so perfectly suited for one another. His touch kindles a fire inside me, and his warm mouth against my skin sends me to heavenly oblivion.

"Are you hungry?" I ask him a long while later.

He lay on his back, smiling with his eyes closed and his arms around me. "I could probably eat a little something."

Raising up, I kiss him and reach for the leather bag containing our lunch. We both sit up, managing to stay covered for the most part, and dine on fried chicken, potato salad, rolls, and pecan pie that I made using my mother's recipe. When Mama passed away three years ago, I brought back her whole collection of recipes. During the times that I'm really missing her, I make one of her recipes and it helps to cheer me up and lift my spirits.

"You thinking about your mama?"

"Yes. Just missing her a little."

"She was a good woman. I miss her, too."

"She adored you and the kids."

"Probably because I'm so adorable."

"Oh. Good grief," I say and he grins. "Your humility grows daily." When his grin widens, I chuckle. Dane has the same grin. In fact, he is almost a carbon copy of his father. So is Maggie. All of our children would have looked like Hayden . . .

Sobering, I finish eating in silence, becoming lost in my own thoughts, no longer able to meet Hayden's eyes. I can't look at him now, because if I do, he will guess my thoughts. I don't want him to know what still fills my mind. But when he places a finger under my chin, urging me to meet his eyes, I realize my efforts have been in vain.

Hayden

Taking Raine's face in his hands, Hayden looks into her tear-filled eyes. He can see her struggling to blink them away and it hurts his heart. Once so confident in herself, Hayden has watched his wife slowly change, and he senses her sadness. She can no longer have children and feels like her importance in being a woman has diminished. She has never come straight out and said it, but then again she doesn't have to. He knows her so well, he can almost sense what she feels at times. They are that in tune with one another.

Hayden has tried to show her that his love for her, and her importance to him and their children will never fade. He is sure she knows this. Never the less, he senses her doubt in her worth. And this is what hurts. To Hayden, there isn't a better wife or mother in the world. He is proud of her and feels blessed to have her as his wife.

"I love you, baby."

I smile, kissing his palm. "I love you too."

"You mean everything to me. You know that, don't you?"

"I know," I answer, mentally chastising myself. Heaving a deep sigh, I do my best to let it go. I pack up the leftovers, and the plates and cups. Then I turn back to Hayden, meeting his lazy smile with my own. "I know that look," I tell him. "It's an 'I'm not ready to go back to work' look."

"You read my mind, darlin'," he says, pulling me back into the blanket and into his arms.

"I'm supposed to be making pies right now for the barbeque tonight," I breathe just as his mouth covers mine.

"We'll go into town and buy some frozen ones," he whispers as his lips trail to my ear, and then back to mine. His kiss deepens, his embrace tightens, and I can think of nothing else.

Chapter 3

I place the freshly-baked pies on the table, hoping no one will be disappointed that they are store-bought. Hayden's heated attentions had taken up a good part of the afternoon and I had ended up making a quick dash to the store. Thinking of him causes a delicious shiver to travel through me.

"I know that smile," Caroline says, placing condiments on the table. "Must have been a good lunch."

A blush heats my cheeks. "It was," I say and she laughs.

Soon the guests begin to arrive, starting with the hired hands, and then Edward and Dawn Henderson and Dean and Audrey Webb. Both couples have been friends of the McKade family for years. I get along with the wives for the most part, but lately Audrey Webb has been drinking a little more than normal, and when she is drunk, she says whatever is in her head with no thought for others. Her husband Dean is a cop and would arrest his wife if he could for being drunk and disorderly. Dean once told Hayden he only stays with her because of the kids. He doesn't want them to have to deal with the instability of a broken home. It is such a sad situation, but I understand why he stays, and I do feel sorry for him.

Today it seems Audrey has already had a few too many. We are not even done with dinner yet and she has hit the loose inhibition stage.

"Did you hear about Cheryl?" she asks, sitting across the patio table from Hayden. I listen to the conversation while collecting the used disposable plates and cups.

"What about Cheryl?" Caroline asks, taking a seat at the table next to Dave.

"She's pregnant with her fifth. I swear that girl is a baby making machine, just like me. Pretty soon they're gonna catch up with me and Dean with our seven."

"That's good for them," Caroline comments, glancing my way. I know she is concerned about my feelings and I force a smile, letting her know I am fine.

"Yeah, I love me some babies," Audrey continued. "So Hayden, when are ya'll gonna have another one?"

Unbelievable! I turn to her, doing my best to mask the hurt, and I feel Hayden's eyes on me, as well as everyone else's.

"Oh, I forgot," Audrey went on, "Raine's missing the parts, isn't she? I'm sorry, that's gotta be tough for you, Hayden, huh?"

Hayden swears softly, anger furrowing his brow.

"Audrey," her husband warns, "you've said enough."

"Well, it has to be tough." She grins. "Bet you'd have fun looking for a surrogate, and I'm sure you'd have no problem finding a volunteer."

"All right," Dean said standing, "let's go." He grabs his wife's hand, pulling her up. "Raine, Hayden, I'm sorry."

Audrey laughs. "Whoops, I guess I've said too much. But hey, Hayden is a good looking man and there are plenty of fertile women who would love to pony up and breed with him."

"What, are you applying for the job?" I ask, tired of listening to her. The 'Raine Attitude' is cutting loose and having its moment. "You think because you *do* have the parts, you're woman enough to 'pony up' with *my* husband and fill in for a job that will never be yours?"

Audrey laughs. "Well, if you insist."

"Shut up, Audrey!" Dean yells. "Just shut up!" Genuine surprise fills her expression and she says nothing else.

"Thanks for dinner." Dean gives me a sympathetic look, mouthing *"I'm sorry."*

"We're glad you could come," I say, taking a deep breath and releasing it slowly. "I'm going to go and check on the kids." I quickly leave, not waiting for a reply. Walking around to the side of the house, I find Dane and Maggie swinging.

"Hey, Mama," Dane says with a wide grin.

Swallowing against the rising emotion, I smile. "Hey, buddy. You being good to your sister?"

"Yeah. Ain't that right, Maggie?"

His little sister grins, exposing the large space where two front teeth should be. "Yeah."

My heart warms and I futilely blink back the tears blurring my vision. In the next moment, Hayden's arms come around me. I turn and cling to him. His embrace tightens and I am no long able to hold my emotions inside. The tears come like a river, soaking the front of his shirt.

"I'm sorry, I whisper against his chest.

"Shhh, you ain't got nothing to be sorry about." His voice is soft. " Audrey is the one with the problem. She can only wish she was half the woman you are. Besides, she's a couple of cans short of a six pack, anyway."

When I snort, a chuckle rumbles in his chest and I laugh. Drawing back a little, I smile up at him. He always knows exactly what to say. "Thanks, I needed that."

Taking my face in his hands, he wipes my tears. Then he kisses me, whispering against my lips, "You are the best thing that has ever happened to me, baby. And because of you, I have the other two cute best things over there. I can't imagine what my life would be like if you hadn't come into it. I can't even think about it." He rests his forehead against mine. "You really are everything to me, Raine," he breathes. "I wouldn't change a thing even if I could. I love you desperately. Nothing else matters."

Wrapping my arms around his neck, I press against him, letting his words penetrate my mind and heart. As we kiss passionately, I vow to let go of the feelings I've carried inside and never think on them again.

After another moment, we grab the kids and head back around the house, almost running into Jack before we even turn the corner.

"Just checking to see if ya'll are all right." His speech is slightly slurred.

"We're fine," Hayden says in a chilling tone I haven't heard him use in years.

"Well, all right then," Jack says, smiling my way. "Thanks for dinner." He tips his hat and heads down to the bunkhouse with the rest of the guys, briefly glancing back at us.

I look up at Hayden and he quickly smiles, but I can feel the tension radiating from him.

When everyone is finally gone, we finish helping Caroline clean up and head home.

Chapter 4

After getting school work done with the kids, I make them lunch and get them settled in for a nap. Making sure they are asleep, I walk down to the stable, deciding that a short ride would do me good.

I enter the stable and find it deserted. Sometimes the men take all the horses out for exercise, and it looks like this is one of those days. I turn to leave when Jack enters.

"Well, hey there, beautiful." His speech is slightly slurred again. Obviously he has been drinking on the job, which is a big no no at the McKade ranch.

"Hello," I say, heading to the door, but he blocks my path.

"Slow down, girl. Where you running off to?"

Seriously? "Let me pass, please."

"No, I wanna talk to you a bit."

"I have no desire to talk to you, so move out of my way."

"I'll tell you what I *desire.* I desire *you.*"

By now I am livid. I'm also a little afraid. "You can't have me."

I try to go around him again, but he grabs my arm. Going with my first instinct, I attempt to send a knee to his groin, but he blocks the blow. I frantically fight to get away from him, but his grip only tightens, causing me pain. He yanks me against him and the smell of alcohol on his breath makes me nauseous. I continue my struggle, doing everything in my power to get away. My fear grows with each second that passes.

"Hayden!" I yell. "Hayden, help me!"

"Stop fighting me, Raine, and stop yelling because no one is close enough to hear you. You know what I want, and I'm gonna have it, whether you wanna give it to me or not." Imprisoning me with one arm, he turns me away from him and slams me back against his chest, the buttons on my shirt flying as he rips it open, and then off. Spinning me back around to face him, he wraps a hand in my hair, yanking my head back, exposing my neck to his repulsive mouth, biting hard enough to leave a mark.

"No!" I continue to struggle, futilely crying out for help, hoping that somehow someone will hear me.

"You know what?" he growls. "I'm tired of this." He slams a fist against my eye and lands another against my cheek. I am dazed and I struggle to focus, but the fight has gone out of me and I begin to whimper. My brain urges me to keep fighting, but my mind says it's hopeless. He finally pulls me into one of the stalls, knocking me against the wall.

Please help me, God, I pray. *Please . . .*

Dragging me to the floor, he pins my arms above my head and my legs under his. Then he begins to unbuckle my belt.

"No!" I cry. The fight in me is revived. He slaps my face hard and continues to undo my jeans. "No," I plead. "Please don't."

Just as I close my eyes and start to accept that all is lost, I am suddenly free of his weight.

Hayden

The sight that meets Hayden's eyes sends him into a fit of rage, causing him to completely snap. A loud profane roar escapes him as he yanks Jack up by the back of his jeans. Pulling him out of the stall, Hayden sends a massive fist to his jaw, the power of it snapping the man's head back. Holding onto the front of Jack's shirt, Hayden lands a punch against his nose, immediately hearing it crack. He picks Jack up, holding him over his head, and throws him against the wall.

"She is my woman!" Hayden yells, storming over to him. "She's mine! You keep your hands off her!" Yanking the battered man up, he beats him even more.

It takes four men to pull Hayden away from Jack, otherwise he would surely kill the man. "Look at me, Hayden!" Tom says standing in front of him. "Go to Raine! She needs you!"

Hayden begins to struggle again, but Tom grabs the front of his blood-stained shirt. "Hayden, go to your wife! We'll take care of Jack! We've already called Dean and he's on his way."

Glowering at the unconscious man on the floor, Hayden takes a calming breath and nods. When he finally speaks, the tone of his voice is ice-cold. "Tell Dean I want that garbage off my property, and if he ever comes back, I'll kill him."

"We'll tell him," Tom said. "Go to Raine."

Pushing a blood-covered hand back through his hair, Hayden heads to the stall. The minute his eyes fall upon Raine lying in the straw, curled up on her side, the rage is replaced by a pain so intense, it literally tears at his heart. Her face is battered, her shirt completely ripped off, her arms bruised.

Hot tears trail down Hayden's face and he is sick inside. "Oh, baby, I'm so sorry," he whispers brokenly, kneeling in the straw. He reaches for her and she cringes from his touch. She whimpers pitifully, her body curled even tighter, shaking violently. Hayden's heart aches so badly, he wants to just curl up beside her and cry like a baby. It's still hard to believe this has happened.

When Hayden had sent one of the workers back to the stable to grab a feed bucket, the last thing he'd expected was to have the man running back to him, saying he had witnessed Jack attacking his wife. Hayden's insides had literally exploded and he raced to the stable. He almost ripped the door off its hinges, and the sound of Raine sobbing caused him to completely lose it. If the workers hadn't pulled him off Jack, Hayden knew he would have committed murder.

Hayden slowly moved closer. "Raine, baby, it's me. It's just me." He timidly places a hand on her arm, afraid she will flinch away from him again. When she doesn't, he slowly turns her over, his eyes filling again at the sight of the extensive bruising on her face. Her left eye is swollen shut, and finger marks mar her shoulders and arms. His eyes move to the large bite mark on her neck and he is unable to stop the sob that escapes him. Taking off his shirt, he covers her and picks some of the hay from her hair.

"Hayden," she finally whispers brokenly, looking up at him. "Hayden," she softly repeats.

"I'm here, darlin'. I'm right here." He carefully lifts her in his arms, cradling her against him. She feels as fragile as a China doll.

"Don't let me go," she whimpers, burrowing herself against his chest. "Don't let me go."

"I'll never let you, go, baby," he promises, pressing his forehead to her. "I'll never let you go."

Chapter 5

*H*ayden carries me into the house. In his arms,

I feel as safe as a child, and when he puts me down, just as terrified. I grab his hand, clinging to it as if my life depended on me holding on.

"It's okay, darlin'. I'm just gonna check on the kids, all right? I promise I won't be long."

"I'll come with you," I whisper, unable to bear being separated from him.

"All right," he agrees, kissing my brow.

Clinging to him, we go upstairs and look in on Dane and Maggie. Both are still asleep, their peaceful expressions mirroring an innocence only a child can possess. Going back down, we stop in the kitchen and Hayden fills a small freezer bag with ice. When we are back in our room, he takes my hand, leading me to the bathroom and fills the tub. I undress and get in, both wincing and sighing as I lower myself into the warm water.

Hayden quietly picks the rest of the hay from my hair. Nothing is said between us, because there is nothing for me *to* say, and I don't think Hayden knows *what* to say. But his being here for me is enough. I take his hand in mine and lightly touch the swollen knuckles, silently thanking God for the strength of those hands. Hayden lets me lower his hand into the water, releasing a sigh of his own.

I hold the small ice pack against my eye, knowing without even looking in a mirror that my face is a sight. A tear slips down my swollen cheek at the thought.

"You're still beautiful," Hayden says, guessing my thoughts.

Saying nothing, I lift his wet hand to my lips. These hands had saved me. The bruised knuckles had inflicted pain on my behalf. Now, I need the touch of these same hands to help me forget.

Emotion welling inside me, I look into his eyes, finding the same emotion etched into his features.

"Make it go away, Hayden," I plead. "Please make the pain go away."

Helping me out of the tub, he wraps a towel around me and holds me close.

"I'll make it go away, baby." He covers the bruises on my arms with gentle hands. "I'll make it go away," he whispers against my brow, carrying me to bed. Once

I am between the cool sheets, cradled in the warmth of his embrace, my body the recipient of his loving and tender caresses, and my mouth and swollen face bathed in the healing balm of his kisses, he truly does make it go away.

As long as I am in his arms, nothing can touch me. Not the pain, nor the memory of it. With the melding of my body to his, the pain fades into nothingness, if only for a short time.

Hayden

As the light of the full moon slips through the blinds, illuminating the bedroom, Hayden holds Raine and silently cries. She lay on top of him, cradled like a child, her head resting on his chest, her face in the curve of his neck, sleeping deeply. After waking earlier, completely terrified, Hayden knew he would have to hold her as close as possible to keep the nightmares away, and decided this would be the best way.

Staring up at the dark ceiling, tears trail back into his hair, falling onto the pillow. He keeps asking himself how this could have happened. *What made that jerk think he had a right to my wife?* Even now, there is still a part of Hayden that wants to find Jack and finish the job.

When Dean had come back from dropping Jack off at the hospital, he said he told Jack not even bother pressing charges because if he did, he would be taken to court for attempted rape. Add that to past charges of abuse–none of them even knew he had–he would most likely serve some time. Dean would see to that.

Hayden sighs deeply, and is again grateful that Tom and the others pulled him off Jack. Otherwise he would be in jail himself, not lying here holding this woman who means more to him than life itself. He just hopes and prays she will be okay and can overcome the emotional trauma Jack's violence had wrought. When Dane and Maggie woke from their naps and saw their mama, both had burst into tears. He and Raine had comforted them the best they could, and Hayden assured them that their mama would be okay and the bad man who hurt her was gone. Hayden promised them he wouldn't ever let anyone hurt their mama again.

And he intends to keep his word.

Hayden finally drifts to sleep with a prayer of fulfilling that promise on his lips.

Chapter 6

I awaken the same way I had fallen asleep–burrowed against Hayden's chest, securely wrapped in his arms. I know he is awake, but I don't move. I just tighten my embrace, never wanting to leave our bed.

But practicality makes me abandon the thought. Dane and Maggie will be awake soon and I need to start breakfast.

"Good morning, baby." Hayden's voice is raspy. His long fingers gently caress my back.

"Good morning." I glance at the clock. He is usually up and ready by now. "You probably need to get going."

"I'm not going down today. They can handle things just fine. I'm gonna stay home with you and the kids today."

There are no words to describe how much having him here means to me, but I can't keep him from doing his job.

"Thanks," I finally say, "but if you need to go I will be fine."

He buries a hand in my hair, holding me close with the other. "The only thing I need, darlin', is to be with you, so don't be feeling guilty. Right now my place is with you. All right?"

I smile. "Okay."

"You want me to hold you a little longer?"

"There is nothing I want more."

We spend most of the morning in the family room with the kids, playing games and watching cartoons. During nap-time, Hayden and I sit on the porch swing, quietly enjoying the sounds of nature and the rustling trees around us.

When nights falls again and Dane and Maggie are tucked into bed, we watch a movie until I am too tired to keep my eyes open. As soon I fall asleep, the nightmare comes back as vivid and fresh as ever. I see everything clearly. I feel Jack's hands gripping my arms and his disgusting mouth on me. I relive each punch and the pain that came with them. I can even smell the alcohol.

I awaken screaming. Then Hayden soothes me with loving caresses. And the merging of his body with mine drives the pain and visions away.

For three days, this pattern continues. I can barely eat during the day because my fear of the night suppresses my appetite.

I haven't been able to return to the stable. Each time I think about it, anxiety seizes me and I can think of nothing except what happened there. And every time I think about poor Hayden and what I am putting him through, my heart aches. I know I need to pull myself together, but I don't know how. I need to get past this, to feel normal again. To feel like *me* again.

Chapter 7

After reading a story to Dane and Maggie and putting them to bed, I go to the kitchen to make sure everything is done. Wiping down the sink, Hayden embraces me from behind and presses a kiss to my ear.

"Come out and sit with me on the swing."

"All right." I grab a quilt from the linen closet.

Wrapping the quilt around us, Hayden rocks the swing gently and we enjoy the night air.

Kissing my temple, he asks, "How would you feel about getting away for a bit? Just the two of us?"

"That sounds wonderful," I answer with a sigh. "Maybe we can talk to Caroline tomorrow about watching the kids."

"I already did, darlin'. It's all arranged."

"Really?"

"Yep. We leave a week from today. Just pack enough clothes for a week."

"Hayden," I breathe, unable to believe what I'm hearing. "Really?"

"Really." He softly caresses my face. "We need this time away."

"Are you going to tell me where we're going?"

He smiles, leaning in to kiss me. "Yeah, as soon as we're on our way to the airport." He fully presses his mouth to mine, producing an instant heat that is as familiar to me as my own name.

A little over one week later.
Pigeon Forge, Tennessee

"What can I get you folks?"

"You know what you want, darlin'?"

"Yes, I would like the BLT with fries and a ginger ale."

"Same for me," Hayden says, handing the waitress our menus.

"All right, I'll get your order in and be back with your drinks."

We thank her and she leaves. Taking my hand, Hayden kisses it and smiles. I smile back, wanting more than anything to be alone with him again, wrapped in the warmth of his arms, in our cabin.

We arrived in Pigeon Ford two days ago and are staying in a cozy, beautiful and roomy log cabin at Eagles Ridge Resort. When I asked Hayden why he picked Pigeon Forge for our vacation, he said it was because he knew how much I've always loved Dolly Parton. I kissed him right there at the ticket counter, drawing smiles from the ticket agent and passengers waiting in line.

Yesterday we spent the whole day at Dollywood and were completely worn out by the time we got back to our cabin. This morning we stayed in bed until late, talking, making love, and talking some more. Now, sitting next to him in a booth at a little country cafe, I feel free and uplifted again. Hayden had been right. We really have needed the time away. The bruises on my face have faded some, which is why we waited to take this trip. Makeup erases what is left.

I casually glance around the cafe, loving the hometown feel of the place. I watch a girl across from our booth as she quickly cleans a table and sets it for the next customer. Her blond hair falls just above the shoulders of her small frame. When she turns, I'm surprised by how young she looks. She can't be more than sixteen or seventeen. Her sky blue eyes stare hauntingly from a pale heart-shaped face. She notices me looking at her and smiles, and her face lights up the cafe. She's beautiful, like an angel.

"How are ya today?" she asks, lifting a tray of dishes and balancing it on her shoulder.

"We're great," I answer, looking at her name tag. "How are you, Joy?"

"I'm good, thanks." Her southern drawl is engaging. "You're not from here, are ya?"

Hayden smiles. "No, we're just visiting."

"From where, if you don't mind my asking?"

"We live in Roswell, New Mexico" She immediately grins and Hayden chuckles.

"Alien country, huh?"

We laugh and Hayden squeezes my hand. "She sounds like you, darlin', when you first came."

"I know. Joy, in the words of my sister-in-law when I moved from Atlanta, "the only aliens in Roswell are the ranch hands after a night of partying. They are usually so green, they look like aliens.""

Joy laughs. "Do you have children?"

"Yes," I answer. "We have a son who is seven and a five-year-old daughter. Unfortunately, we are unable to have more." It feels good to be able to say it without wanting to cry.

"I'm sorry to hear that. I'm sure the good Lord will continue the blessings in some other way."

"I'm sure you're right," I agree.

Joy smiles, adjusting her tray. "Well, I should get back to work."

"It was good to meet you, Joy. I'm Raine and my husband is Hayden.

"I'm please to meet ya'll. If you don't mind me saying, you make a beautiful couple."

I smile. "Thanks, that's sweet of you to say."

"Yeah," Hayden adds, "but just so you know, my wife contributes most of the beauty."

"I understand," she says, laughing again. "I hope you enjoy your stay here."

"I'm sure we will." I watch her walk away and start on another table. "What a sweetheart!"

"She is," Hayden agrees. "She can't be more than sixteen or so."

"That's what I was thinking."

Our food arrives and we enjoy a leisurely lunch. I can't help watching Joy float around the restaurant, cleaning tables. Every now and then, her expression almost seems pain-filled. Then she smiles at someone and it's as if the sun has come out after a heavy rain. Each time it happens, I am amazed.

When the waitress finally brings us the check, I ask for a small envelope. She drops it off on her way to another table and Hayden hands me some cash. I put it in the envelope and write Joy's name on the front, wanting to help out a little because she most likely lives off of tips as well.

After thanking the waitress and telling her how much we enjoyed the meal, we get up to leave, stopping to say goodbye to Joy on our way out.

"Will you be coming in again?" she asks us.

Hayden turns to me. "What do you think, baby?"

"Definitely. The food was so good, I wouldn't mind coming back for lunch tomorrow."

"Great," Joy says, smiling widely. "Tomorrow is my day off. Can I join you?"

"Yes," I quickly answer. "We would love that."

"I'll see you tomorrow, then."

"See you tomorrow."

Chapter 8

We slip into the cafe a little before twelve. Joy is already waiting at a table for us.

"Hey," she says as we walk over.

"Hello." I sit on the booth seat and slide over for Hayden. My concern for Joy is instant. Her skin is so pale, even more so than yesterday. "Are you feeling okay?"

She smiles. "I'll answer that after lunch."

"Then let's hurry up and get some food in you," Hayden says. The tone of his voice may sound light, but I hear his concern as well.

"How are you folks today?" a grandfatherly man asks, approaching our table.

"Good," Hayden replies.

"Raine, Hayden, this is my boss, Rick. He owns the place."

"It's good to meet you," Hayden says, shaking the man's hand.

"It's truly a pleasure to meet you both. Just order whatever you want. It's on the house."

"You don't need to do that," I protest, surprised at the kind gesture.

"Oh, I insist. Any friends of our Joy's are friends of mine."

"That's nice of you," Hayden says.

"No problem. Enjoy your lunch."

"That's so kind of him," I tell Joy. "He must really care about you."

"He does. I have made some great friends here. They're like family."

I give her an understanding nod. "If you don't mind me asking, how old are you?"

"I'm seventeen."

"You got family living close by?" Hayden inquires.

"Nope. This is it."

"How did you wind up here on your own?" I ask.

"It's a long story, but to sum it up, I did some things my parents didn't approve of and they kicked me out. I've been on my own for over a year now."

My eyes meet Hayden's and I know our thoughts are the same. What in the world could she have done that was bad enough for her parents to put her out on the street?

"I know you're wondering," she says with a sad smile. "Their disapproval of me dating guys that were not white was the biggest reason they made me leave."

I can't believe it! But then again, I can, especially here in the south. "But you were only sixteen."

"Yeah, that didn't matter much to my folks."

"Well," Hayden says, "it was their loss."

"Thanks."

"So what's your favorite thing on the menu?" he asks when he sees the waitress coming our way. It is the same young woman who served us yesterday.

"That would be the country omelet with sweet potato pancakes. I call it my anytime meal."

The waitress–she is wearing a name tag today that says Lynn–smiles at Joy.

I chuckle. "That sounds great. Make that two."

"I guess the ladies have spoken," Hayden says with a grin. "Make that three. We'll take some milk and orange juice, too."

"Got it. Three Joy Specials."

"Lynn," Joy says, "meet my new friends, Hayden and Raine."

"Good to officially meet you folks. Any friend of Joy's is a friend of mine."

"That's just what your boss says." I smile. "Hayden and I are honored to call you all friends." For a minute, I could swear there are tears in her eyes.

She quickly turns away, calling over her shoulder, "Be back with your milk and orange juice."

"So, you said you guys live on a ranch?"

"Yes, Hayden and his brother run it. I'm a homemaker, which I totally love."

"I'll bet your children love the ranch."

"They do," Hayden answers.

"And sometimes he takes them out to work with him. I call those times learning experiences. Hayden calls them playtime because that's what he winds up doing most of the time."

When Joy smiles, it doesn't reach her eyes this time, and her expression quickly changes to one of pain.

"Joy, are you all right?" I ask.

"I'll be fine," she whispers. But a couple of seconds later, she falls from her chair.

"Joy!" We jump up and kneel beside her. I press a hand to her forehead. She feels cold and clammy.

"Rick!" both Lynn and I call and he bursts through the kitchen door. "She just fainted," I tell him as tears trail down my face. "What's wrong with her? She looks so sick today."

Rick raises his watery gaze to us. "Hayden, would you pick her up and carry her for us?"

"Of course. Where are we taking her?"

"Just follow me."

Chapter 9

We follow Hayden and Lynn through the kitchen and out one of the two doors in the back. We walk down a short hallway and Rick opens another door to a cozy apartment, beautifully decorated in country decor.

"Back here," Rick says and we follow him to one of the small bedrooms. Hayden gently places her on the bed and Rick takes off her shoes and covers her with a soft quilt. Leaning down, he presses a hand to her cheek and her eyes slowly open.

"I guess I ruined lunch, huh?" She slowly smiles.

I sit on the edge of the bed, covering her small hand with mine. She gives it a weak squeeze. "You did no such thing," I say, flicking a tear away and forcing a smile. "We're so worried about you."

Joy's eyes move to Rick and Lynn, and something unspoken passes between them.

"Lynn and I will be back in a bit." Rick bends and kisses her cheek, whispering something in her ear before taking Lynn's hand and leading her from the room. He closes the door.

"Come closer," she tells me. I scoot closer to the head of the bed, making room for Hayden to sit beside me. "I need to talk to you about something."

"Okay," I say, squeezing her hand, my heart aching as I watch tears trail back into her hair.

"I prayed you here."

Hayden and I glance at each other. "What do you mean, sugar?" he asks.

She sighs deeply. "I mean I prayed for you to come." Glancing at my confused expression, she goes on. "I have cancer. I've had it for almost nine months and I've been grateful for each new day I have been given. But I'm afraid I don't have many more days."

"Oh, Joy," I cry brokenly. "Why didn't you tell us?"

"Because I wanted to get to know you first. I thought I would have a little more time. I . . . I need to ask something of you."

"What is it?" Hayden asks, his eyes moist. "You can ask us anything."

Joy gives us both a sad smile. "What I'm about to ask you is the very reason I prayed you here."

We turn as the door opens. A small gasp escapes me and I cover my mouth with one hand and squeeze Hayden's hand with the other. I pull my eyes away from the doorway, meeting Joy's beautiful teary smile. "This is why I prayed you here."

Rick and Lynn enter the bedroom, each of them holding a sleeping baby in their arms.

"This little lady is Liesl," Rick says, opening the pink blanket, exposing the adorable, one-month-old infant.

"And this handsome fellow is Kurt," Lynn says, opening the blue blanket covering Liesl's twin. "Our Joy is a big Von Trapp fan and considers *The Sound of Music* the greatest movie ever made."

"My idea of the perfect family," Joy says. Her voice is weak. She looks at Rick and Lynn and they nod, handing one baby to me and the other to Hayden.

"The babies' biological father is black, and he dumped me before I could even tell him I was pregnant, which turned out to be a good thing. After I found out I was pregnant and moved to Pigeon Forge was when I learned of the cancer. Besides not having health insurance, I couldn't undergo treatments because they would have affected the babies and I could not put their lives at risk." She pauses, her voice cracking with emotion. "I needed a kind, loving couple who would be willing to take my babies into their hearts and home, and love them unconditionally. I know God has chosen you. Please say you will take them."

Tears trickle down my cheeks as I gaze down at the beautiful little boy in my arms, and then at his equally beautiful sister. "But why us?" I ask softly.

"Because I prayed, and you came into the cafe. From the moment I saw your motherly smile, and then witnessed Hayden's love for you, I knew you were the couple the good Lord wanted to take my children and give them a loving home. My parents don't know they exist, and I don't want them to. I want these babies to have so much more than I did." She pauses, grimacing as her pain increased. "Please say you will take them."

Hayden and I look at one another, each of us knowing our thoughts are the same. I turn back to Joy. "It would be an honor and a privilege to care for your children as our own. We love them already."

The young girl smiles widely. "Thank you." She lifted a hand, gesturing to the dresser. "Rick?" He picks up a folded piece of paper and a large yellow envelope.

"Rick typed this up for me. He and Lynn are here to witness the legal handing over of Liesl and Kurt to you. Just sign the paper and they will add their signatures."

As I watch Hayden transfer Liesl to one arm and sign the paper, I marvel that we are being blessed with such an amazing opportunity. During all the time I've mourned my lost ability to have more babies, God has had a plan of His own in motion.

I sign below Hayden's signature and hand the paper back to Rick. He and Lynn sign and he gives Hayden the signed document along with the envelope.

"This is a packet of legal information about the babies, birth certificates and things like that."

My heart is so full at this moment, I can scarcely take it all in. I turn back to Joy. "What can we do for you? Is there anything you want or need?"

"Could you just stay with me for a while?"

"Just try to make us leave," I say, drawing a small laugh from her.

Rick and Lynn bring in lunch for us. We eat and talk with Joy about the babies, as well as Dane and Maggie, speculating about their future and the kind of people they will grow up to be. We share both laughter and tears all afternoon. Then night falls and the sunlight fades, taking Joy's strength with it.

The next morning, with the four of us surrounding her, and the twins cuddled in her arms, Joy slips away peacefully, and though Hayden and I have only known her for two short days, we mourn her loss as deeply as Rick, Lynn, and the rest of the staff. In some ways, I think her loss is even more devastating to us, because she loved and trusted us enough to leave her precious babies in our care. In doing this, she gave us her heart.

And we will never break it. Her loving sacrifice will be remembered and treasured forever.

Epilogue

Ten years later.

While Hayden, Dane and Kurt get washed up and changed after working the ranch, Maggie and Liesl help me fill the picnic basket with the lunch we've prepared for our road trip to Disneyland. Hayden and I never made it back there after our honeymoon, and we figure it's time we did. The kids are excited and have talked of nothing else all week.

Once we have everything loaded into the SUV, we round up the kids and hit the road. With my hand tucked in Hayden's, I contemplate all I've been blessed with. I have four beautiful children, all of whom bring me joy and fill our home with laughter. I am privileged to be a stay at home mom and I never want for anything, neither do our children.

And I have the most loving and wonderful husband I could possibly ask for.

I stare at his profile while he drives, taking in his handsome features. His thick chestnut hair is graying at the temples, as well as his short beard, but he is still beautiful, both inside and out, and a simple look or touch from him still warms my blood. Not a day goes by that I don't feel gratitude for my decision to come to New Mexico to live with Dave and Caroline, because the move led me to Hayden.

I often think back on my life before coming to Roswell. I had a career that afforded me a luxurious life, and I had been married to a man with the means to keep me in that luxury. Some would say I had it all.

But truthfully, I had nothing. Not compared to what I have now.

Now, I have everything. In place of worldly riches is the love of my husband and children. And I finally know my true worth.

That knowledge, more than anything else, is what I treasure most.

Author Bio

J. (Jewel) Adams stays crazy busy with her family and writing. She has written several books in different genres and is also a motivational speaker to both youth and adult audiences. She home schools her four kids that are still at home, and between that and conjuring up new ideas for her books, her brain is completely fried most of the time. She and her husband Sean are the parents of eight children, which means they are both losing hair, but hey, that's what Rogaine is for, right?

In her spare time (when she has any) she likes to curl up with a good book and a healthy stash of orange Tic Tacs. She and her family reside in Utah.

Jewel loves hearing from her fans, so if you would like to contact her to tell her how much you love her books or give her sympathy for the fried brain, or suggestions for the hair loss problem (for her husband, of course) contact her at **jewela40@gmail.com**

Website: **JewelAdams.com**

Blog: **jewelsbestgems.blogspot.com**

Other books by J. Adams/Jewel Adams
The Legacy
The Wishing Hour
Guardian of My Heart
Tears of Heaven
Place In This World
Forbidden Portals: The Quicksilver Project
The Journey
Against the Odds
Mercedes' Mountain
Stories of the Heart – A Christmas Short Story Collection
Ebooks
The Wishing Hour
The Legacy
Tears of Heaven
Place In This World: The Sequel to The Journey
The Journey
Mercedes' Mountain
For Love of Angel (PDF only)
Elise's Heart (PDF only)
Children's Book
Forbidden Portals: The Quicksilver Project
The Shelter of His Arms – A Passionate Hearts Novelette
What the Heart Sees – A Passionate Hearts Novelette

*All Books Are Also Available in Kindle and Nook Versions (Elise's
Heart and Mercedes' Mountain, and For Love of Angel excluded)*